Friday
Moira Tighe

I have lived so long
touched nothing. I   1
the bin, then folded myself away ... p
before he entered. I did not lie for hours in his bath, my hair
floating like seaweed. Not in the days before I learnt where
the borders lay and the freedom to be found within them. He
would do the usual things, work, eat, wash, read. No one
came.

He would stand on the balcony and smoke a single
cigarette, last thing at night. Why are we drawn to the cliff, to
look down to the sea crashing against rocks below?

I took one of his cigarettes, wet it between my lips,
replaced it in the packet.

Once, sunbathing on the balcony, the door slammed shut.
I waited for the evening. He stepped out, looking across to
the east, as I knew he would. I slipped inside, unseen.

At dawn, the rain began to lash. He left and I looked out to
see what he looked for on the horizon. Inside was no longer
enough when there was outside.

I curled up beneath his bed and slept. I woke to the sound
of his key in the door. I lay beneath him, as he lay and wrote
his journal. His pencil fell to the floor. As he rolled to retrieve
it, I pushed the pencil to meet his searching fingers. For an
instant we touched the same object. My fingers flew from it.

His breath stilled. As he breathed out, I breathed in. I no
longer knew my own name.

Today, I stepped from the bath and left one wet footprint
on the slate floor. If he returns at the usual time, he'll know.

New World

Fiona Ritchie Walker

She climbs the steps to where I'm waiting at the door. I smile,
point to the table and chairs, fetch water, for she shakes her
head when I show her coffee, tea.

Our only language is a smile, which I send and she catches,
each keeping half as we muddle through the form. I hold up
sheets of pictures. She nods at kettle, microwave, points to rice,
chickpeas.

It's hard to explain tinned steak and kidney pie, instant mash,
can of mushy peas. Her eyes light up at tins of tomatoes and fish

I tick items on the single person list, wonder where she is
living, who is missing.

While we wait for her three day food supply to arrive, I take
her to the extras table, which we used to call treats, until we
started adding toilet roll, shampoo, deodorant to the chocolate
and crisps.

There are plastic-wrapped loaves of soft, white bread. I want
to offer her a fresh-baked seeded crust, but that's in my bread
bin at home.

My own shopping from the market is under my seat in the
welcome area, and I'm quick, picking the brown paper bag and
offering her the sweet, ripe mango that has travelled so far to
reach these shores.

Her hand stretches out, hesitates. I nod, watch her fingers
cup the blush skin as she breathes it in.

She is still for such a long time, I worry at the memories this
fruit carries. She says a word in a language I don't understand.
The two of us are smiling.

Winter sun pours through the stained glass window, turns
teardrops on her eyelashes into rubies and diamonds.

Establishing Connection
Lawrence Sullivan

The satellite dish spun around – searching for some semblance of a signal. Jacob knew that the very second it succeeded, his inbox would be inundated with imploring messages from his father, all begging him to come back home.

Those messages would remain unanswered.

Being on a desert island – devoid of anything other than vast deposits of rhodium – didn't initially feel like Jacob's ideal home either, even if it was only for a few months. The company needed someone to survey the land, and that someone happened to be him.

At first it seemed that the short straw had been drawn.

As time wore on, though, and the waves continued to lap lazily over the shore, that feeling had begun to erode. Waking every morning to a chorus of birdsong instead of a discord of bustling traffic was changing him. Under his feet, asphalt had given way to sand. At night the stars soothed him to sleep, streetlights no longer blazed insistently outside his window. This island was another world.

The lure of generous recompense had originally made Jacob agree to this exploratory expedition. Now it was the experience itself that appeared priceless.

To his surprise, when his web browser had finished refreshing, it wasn't his father's emails that greeted him.

It was head office.

Jacob's line manager was asking for an update. They expected him to submit a full report by the end of the month, then a boat would be dispatched to spirit him back home.

That didn't seem possible, not when he was already there.

Gently closing the laptop, Jacob stood up and carried it to the shoreline. Drinking in the sea air, he pulled the computer back as far as he could and threw it into the ocean.

He would never be forced off his island.

True Stories
Sarah McPherson

She leaned over the rail, watching the waves dance against the hull.

'Careful!'

Her father caught her arm. Grudgingly she stepped back. 'Are we nearly there?'

'An hour, maybe.'

In an hour she would see the island of her grandpa's stories. She had seen it so many times in her mind's eye, loved listening to him talk when the mood took him. Some days he didn't want to, when the memories seemed too raw and speaking of it brought that look into his eyes that made her sad. Other days though, he could spin tales for hours about the beach where he washed up, the things he found. The things he did to survive.

Now she was older she wasn't sure she believed it all. But her parents said it was true – the wreck and the island, anyway. Now they were out here on holiday and had chartered a boat, and soon she would see for herself.

It shimmered into sight over the horizon, looming out of the blue water like something on a postcard. Smaller than she expected, it didn't look big enough to contain everything that grandpa said had happened. They disembarked onto a spit of white sand, and walked around the beach. Her father had a scribbled map, and pointed out things as they went; the fresh water spring that saved Grandpa's life, the rocky outcrop where he built his signal fire.

She ran ahead when she saw the cave mouth. When they caught up she was staring at the rock wall where a series of scratch marks – barred gates – adorned the stone. There were a lot of them. Silently she slipped her hand into her father's and he squeezed it.

'Here?' he said.

She nodded. Her mother handed her the urn.

SURVIVAL
Mavis Pilbeam

'I thought I was done for!' A burst of incredulous, unsympathetic laughter.

'It's no joke. A 60-footer coming…If I'd had time to think, I'd've been wondering how I'd manage building that shelter.'

'Oh, like your namesake.'

'Exactly,' replied Chris Robinson, just back from a round-the-world voyage, single-handed. 'I'd've had my choice of desert islands, I can tell you.'

A dozen heads peer round the door, are stared at and withdraw to the next room.

* * * * * * * * * * * *

TITLE PAGE
WHAT TO DO
If you find yourself
One in a group of a dozen people
On a cold wet windy day
In a historic corner of London,
Invited to sit in a pub with a coffee
And write a Story.

What to do indeed! Stranded. Ingenuity desperately stretched. Something must turn up! Look, smell, taste, touch, listen. Aah!

A conversation through the wall punctuated by laughter.

LIST
DIFFERENT WAYS OF LAUGHING
A hearty, appreciative haw haw.
A ladylike, muffled sniff.
A tearing, humourless screech.
A series of pretty titters.
An embarrassing snorting splutter.
A long yacking hack.

Ears straining to hear what calls forth these ridiculous, so human sounds, muse on the fact that no other animals on Earth laugh.

****

'My namesake had three.'

'If I had a parrot I would teach it to laugh.'

'I once met a mynah bird that laughed. It could wolf-whistle too.'

But that's another story.

CONCLUSION
Something always turns up.

COURT REPORT
Jonathan Fox

Central Courthouse, Sheffield.

The millionaire and yeast-fermentation mogul, Casper Salmon, is still pursuing his £25 million legal action against the luxury tour operator 'Robinson's Cruises'. He's claiming damages against the firm for 'extreme distress and physical torture' after he was unintentionally stranded on his own desert island for more than 100 days.

Until 2011 Robinson's Cruises operated a holiday service that invited customers to 'experience their very own Robinson Crusoe adventure', whereby 'lucky' travellers would be stranded on their own remote pacific island for a 2-week break. The adventurers would be given detailed survival instructions and left to fend for themselves, aping the Defoe novel. Mr. Salmon and his 'Man Friday', former secretary Gillian Mangrove, were two such willing participants of the unusual getaway. Unfortunately, during their stay, the cruise company went into administration, making the desertion all too real for the couple. As 'panic' overtook the London offices, the error was never spotted. During this period several people were simultaneously made redundant – including the agents for Mr. Salmon and Miss Mangrove.

Mr. Salmon, a notorious recluse, was not reported missing back home, nor was Miss Mangrove who had recently walked out on her estranged husband and had made it clear to her family and friends that she didn't want to be contacted during this difficult period.

Unhappily for her, those wishes were granted. It wasn't until months later that the error was identified by the companies' administration company.

The lawsuit was initially contested as Mr. Salmon had signed a waiver that disassociated Robinson's Cruises from actions beyond their control. 'It's all part of the adventure,' said an outgoing spokesperson for the company, who also added, 'at least they got rescued. It's all quite romantic really.'

The case will be heard again next month. Mr. Salmon was unavailable for comment.

The Return
Nora Nadjarian

Footsteps lead me back to the beginning, to where it all started, like a criminal returning to the scene of a crime.

I taught myself, a million years ago, to see in the dark. I learned to understand silence, to hold onto nothing. I swam to the bottom of the sea, to the end of that other world, looking for companionship, when things became unbearable. A diver in search of shipwrecked souls, my heart pounded, my head turned, my mind raced ahead of me, my flesh turned blue. But I always came back to the surface just in time. It was on one of those occasions that the thought came to me – that if I created them, if I wrote it all down, it might come true.

When they invite me to give talks about my adventure, I point the red laser light at the screen, and never know whether I should tell them the truth or not. I point at slides of hand-written pages, of watercolour paintings: part of a hut, bones on the beach, my umbrella, Pol's plumage, Friday's face – and as the red light burns patterns and I recount incidents I've carefully selected, my voice trembles. My hand shakes, and I feel I'm playing a game with my own conscience. Somewhere in the past a parrot shrieks: *Liar, liar, liar.*

'Are you all right, Mr Crusoe?'

'Yes, thank you. A little dizzy, that's all.'

'What do you miss the most?'

'Friday's voice, when he first spoke.'

'Would you ever go back?'

I would. And I'd write the same story, but told from Friday's point of view. I miss him dearly. There was not another soul on the island and I had to create him. I had to create it all.

Reaping

Elizabeth Forsyth

When the first button fell off he blamed his hands; too clumsy. When the second came off he blamed the washer; too hot. When the third came off he blamed the manufacturer; too cheap. He yelled for his wife, a worn out figure who came scurrying in her black dress with a sewing kit.

'Fix it,' he said.

His wife took the buttons and, one by one, sewed them back on while he still wore the shirt. A vertical line of red dots followed her needle; one behind each button. With each prick of the needle he said 'ouch', never 'thank you'. He said 'hurry up' and 'I could do this faster', though he didn't know how to sew.

'How could you do this to me?' he asked.

She snipped loose threads with practiced precision. He took the scissors out of her hands and cut the threads to one button that had been sewed back on slightly crookedly. It fell into his palm and he handed it over to her. 'Again,' he said.

Sarah McPherson
Sarah McPherson is a writer of short fiction and poetry from Sheffield in the UK, and can be found on Twitter as @summer_moth.

Jon Fox
Jon Fox is a copywriter and part-time author who lives with his wife, record collection and ever-growing wariness of the world around him.
@boredomdespair

Elizabeth Forsyth
Elizabeth Forsyth is an expat who resides in London and thinks a lot about the correct spelling of civilisation.
@Write_Stuff_

Moira Tighe
Flâneuse.

Laurence Sullivan
Runner-up in the Wicked Young Writer Awards, Laurence Sullivan's fiction has appeared in such places as: *Londonist*, *The List* and *Crack the Spine*.
www.laurencesullivan.co.uk
www.facebook.com/LaurenceSullivanWriter

Mavis Pilbeam
Mavis Pilbeam has published some non-fiction and a few poems and is pleased now to have a short story published: a novel next perhaps?